The Curse of Captain Cross-eyed

WeirDStreet

The Curse of Captain Cross-eyed

Margaret Ryan
Illustrated by Kate Pankhurst

A & C Black • London

For Angus and Granny Elspeth with love

First published 2009 by
A & C Black Publishers Ltd
36 Soho Square, London, W1D 3QY

www.acblack.com

Text copyright © 2009 Margaret Ryan
Illustrations copyright © 2009 Kate Pankhurst

ISBN 978-1-4081-0439-2

A CIP catalogue for this book is available from the British Library.

This book is produced using paper that is made from wood
grown in managed, sustainable forests. It is natural, renewable and
recyclable. The [...] form
to the e[...] [...] in.

The problem: My old bike. I am growing too big for it, but we can't afford a new one as Dad is off work with a broken leg.

The brainwave: Ask Mr Maini at the corner shop if he has a paper round so I can save up for some new wheels.

The dilemma: There is a paper round, but it takes in Weir Street and I've heard that the people who live there are weird.

The hero: Me, of course. Jonny Smith. I'm not scared – it's only a paper round. And just how weird can the people in Weir Street be…?

Chapter One

It was the first day of my new job, and I was up really early. Well, not as early as Mum and Dad and Ellie. Ellie's my little sister. Little sisters should be cute, right? Not Ellie. If she's not yelling, she's eating. Everything in sight. Noggin, our cat, gives her a wide berth, ever since she nibbled his tail. And Mum's put Jaws, the goldfish, up on a high shelf, just in case.

I got to the breakfast table just in time to find Ellie with her fingers in the jam and her beady eyes on my toast. She stretched out a sticky, plump hand…

"Leave!" I said, the way I speak to Brutus. That's our dog. I snatched my toast from under her greedy little gaze and headed for the door.

"Good luck, Jonny," called Mum from the kitchen.

"And don't be late for school," shouted Dad, scratching the itchy bits inside his plaster with a knitting needle. He's a community policeman and hates being off work.

"Don't worry, I won't," I called, already half-out the door. "Miss Dodds'll kill me if I'm late again," I muttered to myself.

Miss Dodds knows every excuse under the sun, and won't accept any of them. I know. I've tried often enough. She's got this special kind of teacher's eye that can staple your tongue to your cheek with just one look. And she thinks my head is full of nothing but football.

I ran out to the shed, grabbed my bike, and pedalled off to the corner shop.

Mr Maini was standing behind the counter with a large orange bag full of newspapers.

"Good morning, Jonny," he smiled. "You're in good time. Look, I've marked on the numbers for you. Be careful to deliver each paper to the right house. The numbers in Weir Street can be a bit … weird."

"I've heard the people can be a bit weird, too," I said. "That's why everybody calls it *Weird* Street, and the paperboys don't last."

"People are people," shrugged Mr Maini, and said no more.

That worried me. What *was* it about Weird Street?

I slung the heavy bag over my shoulder and got on my bike. It was harder to cycle carrying the papers and my knees kept banging on the handlebars. I managed to miss most of the traffic, though, by scooting along back alleyways, then freewheeling down Barr Avenue till I met the junction with Weird Street.

That's when the trouble began…

For a start, Weird Street is a steep hill and pedalling up it was a real struggle. For another thing, I nearly fell off my bike several times as I turned my head to look at all the strange houses. Houses are houses, right? Windows, walls, the occasional door. Not in Weird Street. In Weird Street all the houses are different.

My first stop was at house number 34 and a half. It is set right back into the hill. It has bottle-bottom windows and an old oak door covered in iron studs. The garden is full of junk, while on the flat roof there are dozens of neatly planted rows of potatoes. You don't expect to see vegetables where chimneys should be!

A chimney was all I *could* see of the next house. I propped my bike up against its high hedge, opened the squeaky gate and crept through the shoulder-high grass.

It was quiet and eerie with only the odd, soft rustling. Could there be wild animals lurking there? I caught a flick of what looked like a tiger's tail, so I threw the paper in the direction of the house and left, sharpish.

Fortunately, I didn't see anything unusual on the next few deliveries and I was feeling happier as I pedalled further up the hill to number 57. Its garden was very neat and tidy, with every plant standing to attention. Everything looked quite ordinary, if you didn't count the stone Viking warrior fiercely guarding the water butt. I breathed a sigh of relief and popped the paper through the gleaming brass letter box. Yikes, it snapped back and nearly took my fingers off!

The worst was reserved for number 13. Unlucky for some. Number 13 had a crazy, dancing parrot looking out of the window, and a one-eared cat sitting on the doorstep. But no letter box.

So I knocked on the door.

Silence.

I knocked again.

More silence. Then the clump of heavy boots sounded along the hallway. It was scary. Finally, a little porthole window in the front door opened and a loud voice boomed out.

"WHO GOES THERE? FRIEND OR FOE?"

Chapter Two

Friend or foe? Help! I hadn't expected that. What could I say?

"Er ... paperboy," I muttered.

"A boy made out of paper? How very strange. Don't you blow away in the wind?"

"Paper delivery boy," I tried again.

"Then where is the paper?"

I held it up and a hook came out of the porthole to get it. Startled, I let the paper drop, and the door opened.

A large pirate was standing there. "I am Captain Cross-eyed," he bellowed. "Who are you?"

"J-J-Jonny. Jonny Smith."

"Pleased to make your acquaintance, Jonny Smith," he said, and held out his hook.

I gulped and shook the hook. It came away in my hand.

Captain Cross-eyed gave a great belly laugh, then his real hand slid down his sleeve and took the hook back from me. "Good trick, Jonny Smith. Don't you agree?"

I wasn't going to disagree with a huge pirate, so I just nodded. Then I turned and ran down the path. I jumped on my bike and pedalled away fast, only stopping to hand in my orange bag to Mr Maini.

"Did you know that an enormous pirate lives at 13 Weird Street?" I gasped.

"A pirate? In Weir Street? What kind of crazy boy are you? Mr Cross lives at number 13. Nice man. Works in the sausage factory. Now, don't be telling silly stories, Jonny Smith."

It was clear Mr Maini did not believe me.

I jumped on my bike again and headed for school. When I got there though, the playground was empty, except for a crisp packet blowing in the wind.

"Oh no," I groaned. "Late again. Miss Dodds will never believe I was held up by a gigantic pirate."

I was right.

"A large, huge, enormous, gigantic pirate? That's certainly one of your more inventive excuses, Jonny Smith," she said, looking down her long nose at me. "You can stay behind at break and write out the whole fantastic story."

I sighed and went to my desk. The day was getting worse. First Mr Maini didn't believe me, now it was Miss Dodds. *And* I had a story to write. Miss Dodds knew I always played football at break, and she knew that the inter-schools' final was coming up soon…

I slumped down in my seat.

"A large, huge, enormous, gigantic pirate?" parroted my pal, Sara, nudging my elbow. "Good excuse, Jonny."

"The best yet," agreed Surinder, who was sitting behind me.

"It's not an excuse," I whispered. "There *was* a big pirate. The people in Weird Street are *weird*."

As they picked up their pencils, I could tell from their grins that Sara and Surinder didn't believe me, either.

ഐᎧᏇ

Neither did Mum and Dad when I told them about it after school.

"What an imagination you have, Jonny," smiled Mum, handing me the cutlery to set the table for tea.

"It'll get you into trouble one day," warned Dad. "I happen to know Ian Cross. He manages the sausage factory and very kindly donated several boxes of bangers for the children's barbeque last summer."

"Sossiz, sossiz," grinned Ellie.

"I'm telling the truth," I protested, as Mum ladled tomato soup into bowls. "There really was a pirate."

But no one was listening.

I sat down at the table and picked up my spoon. It's been the weirdest day of my life,

I thought, and no one believes me. However, I was determined to stick with the paper round. I wasn't going to give up like the other paperboys. I was also determined to show everyone I was telling the truth about the pirate. The question was, *how*?

Chapter Three

The idea came to me as I was getting dressed the following morning.

"It's simple," I said. "Why didn't I think of it before?"

I would take my mobile phone and photograph Captain Cross-eyed when I handed over his paper. Then I'd have a picture to prove my story was true.

The only problem was I'd then have to take my phone to school, and Miss Dodds had banned them. One morning, everyone in the class had played the 'psycho' ring tone when she'd arrived. BIG MISTAKE. Still, if my phone was switched off, she'd never know, would she?

I grabbed a quick bowl of cereal, dodging the bits of soggy crusts Ellie threw at me. Then I set off for Mr Maini's.

He was busy in the back of the shop when I arrived and gave me a wave as I collected my papers. "Perhaps you'll see dinosaurs in Weir Street today, Jonny Smith," he laughed.

I felt for my phone and switched it on. Just wait, Mr Maini, you'll see, I thought.

But he didn't, and neither did I.

When I arrived at number 13, I was all ready to take the photo, but there was no sign of Captain Cross-eyed. Or his parrot. Or his cat.

I knocked at the door.

Nothing.

I knocked at the door again.

Still nothing. I even sneaked round to the back garden.

No one. Unless you counted the garden

gnome fishing beside the wheelie bin.

Disappointed, I left the paper under a large stone and went on my way. So much for my big idea. But I wasn't late for school, so Miss Dodds wasn't able to give me a telling off … till my phone rang.

"There's an ice-cream van in the playground!" cried Peter Ho.

Everyone rushed to the window to look. Everyone except me. I knew my ring tone when I heard it. I gasped and quickly switched off my phone.

But I was too late. Miss Dodds had spotted me. "Sit down, everyone," she ordered. "Jonny Smith, bring that phone over here. You know I do not allow them in the classroom. I hope there's a good reason why you have it with you."

I could hardly tell her I was hoping to photograph the pirate she didn't believe I'd seen yesterday, could I?

So I didn't.

"No good reason," I said instead.

"Very well. The phone will stay in my desk for the rest of the week, and you will spend your break doing an extra maths exercise."

That meant no football practice *again*. The other boys in the team glared at me.

"Sorry," I mouthed. I sighed. I'd be lucky to play in the final at this rate.

Sara and Surinder looked at me sympathetically, and at break, they stayed behind to help me with the maths.

"Why did you bring your phone in?" asked Sara. "You know how crazy Miss Dodds went about the 'psycho' thing."

"I wanted to get a photo of the pirate in Weird Street," I muttered.

"You're not *still* on about that, are you?" said Surinder. "Pirates live in books, or in films, not in a street near you, Jonny."

"This one does," I insisted. "He lives in Weird Street and I'll prove it. Just you wait and see."

I thought about the problem all day. I even thought about it during football practice after school. Which was a mistake.

"Smith! Keep your eye on the ball," yelled Mr McGregor, our coach. "You're playing like a big tumshie."

Tumshie is the Scottish word for turnip, so clearly Mr McGregor wasn't very pleased with me. But it was worse than that.

"What's up with you, laddie?" he asked after the game. "Have you forgotten what your feet are for?"

"No," I muttered. "Just got something on my mind."

"Well, get it off your mind or you're off the team. O.K.?"

Very much *not* O.K. I cycled home feeling miserable. I'd lost my mobile phone and almost lost my place in the football team. What was going to happen next?

Chapter Four

"You've to take Ellie and Brutus for a walk," said Dad, when I got home. "Mum didn't have time. Gran's poorly so she's gone over to see her."

"Oh no!" I groaned. Pushing Ellie's pram around was *so* uncool. But, with Dad out of action, there was nothing else for it.

Ellie stopped chewing the ear of her pink rabbit just long enough for me to put on her shoes and coat.

"Eets. Eets," she grinned, as I strapped her into the pushchair.

"No sweets," I said sternly. "You're fat enough. Walkies," I nodded to Brutus, who was hovering hopefully nearby.

He wagged his tail and we set off along the road.

We reached Mr Maini's corner shop and that gave me an idea. I could take Ellie and Brutus for their walk along Weird Street. That way I could try to catch a glimpse of Captain Cross-eyed.

"You're a genius, Jonny Smith," I said.

And it *was* a good idea when I was whizzing the two-ton toddler *down* Barr Avenue, but not when I had to push her *up* Weird Street.

"How would you like to pull the pushchair up the hill, like a husky?" I asked Brutus.

But he just ignored me, and lifted his leg on the big three-wheeler bike parked outside number 34 and a half.

"That bike's even older than mine," I said.

At last I made it to number 13. I knelt by the chestnut tree at the front gate and pretended to be fixing my shoe while I checked out the house.

But there was no one around.

Oh well, it had been worth a try, I thought, and was just about to leave when I spotted something. I backed against the tree. A man had appeared at an upstairs window. He was wearing a black jacket and a three-cornered hat. On his shoulder sat a dancing parrot and, on the end of his arm, I could clearly see a gleaming hook.

It was Captain Cross-eyed!

"Look, Ellie. Look, Brutus," I whispered. "It's him. It's the pirate!"

Ellie looked up and pointed. "Pi," she said, pleased.

"That's right. Pirate. Good girl."

The figure disappeared and, though I waited a little longer, there was no further sign of him. "Probably swinging in his hammock, drinking his rum ration and eating his weevily biscuits," I told Ellie.

I turned the pushchair round and, with Brutus at my heels, headed for home. But at least I had seen Captain Cross-eyed again. At least I knew I hadn't imagined him.

"Now you can tell everyone you've seen the pirate, too," I said to Ellie.

"Pi," she agreed.

When we got home, Dad was setting the table for tea. "Oh, good, you're back," he said, opening the oven. "Mum's been delayed. We'll start eating without her."

I wasn't listening. "Guess what," I said excitedly. "We walked to Weird Street and I saw the pirate again. He was at an upstairs window and was wearing a black jacket and a three-cornered hat and..."

Dad put on his stern, policeman's face. "Are you still on about this pirate nonsense?"

"It's not nonsense, Dad. It's true. Ask Ellie. She saw him, too. Didn't you, Ellie?"

Ellie beamed and pointed at the dish in Dad's hand. "Pi," she said.

"That's right," smiled Dad. "Steak pie. My favourite. Now, let's sit down and eat. And I don't want to hear any more of this rubbish."

I sat down, and Dad served up the pie. Ellie's greedy eyes gleamed at the sight of it and Brutus sat beside me looking hopeful. But I was too annoyed to enjoy the food.

"I *did* see the pirate," I whispered to Brutus. "I wish people would believe me. It's a pity you haven't learned to talk yet..."

Chapter Five

We were *supposed* to be doing silent reading in class the next day, but I was busy thinking about Captain Cross-eyed. I kept a careful eye on Miss Dodds as I took out a piece of paper and started to set down the facts the way Dad had shown me.

THE CASE OF THE MYSTERIOUS PIRATE

FACT 1   Captain Cross-eyed the pirate exists. I know. I've seen him.

FACT 2   Mr Maini knows the owner of 13 Weird Street as McCross who works in the sausage factory.

FACT 3   Dad knows the same man as Ian Cross, the factory manager.

FACT 4   Someone called I. Cross exists.

Then it hit me.

I. Cross. Or Cross I. Or Cross-eyed, alias Captain Cross-eyed. They were obviously all the same person.

"Why didn't I realise before?" I said out loud.

"Why didn't you realise *what* before, Jonny?" snapped Miss Dodds. She was at her desk doing some school reports and hated being disturbed.

"Er, silent reading," I said, quickly hiding the piece of paper. "It's very good."

Miss Dodds fixed me with her steely gaze. "Then do it silently. The clue is in the word *silent*."

"Yes, Miss Dodds," I said excitedly. "Thank you." She didn't know it, but she had just been very helpful. That was what I needed. *Clues*. Clues to the existence of Captain Cross-eyed.

But where would I find them?

I thought for a moment. What would a *real* detective do?

He would search Captain Cross-eyed's wheelie bin! There were bound to be clues there... Empty rum bottles, weevily biscuits, parrot feathers... But I was going to need help if I was to do it without being seen. I looked over at Sara and Surinder and smiled. What are friends for?

Sara and Surinder weren't so keen.

"You want us to help search a smelly wheelie bin for pirate rubbish?" said Sara, when I asked them at break.

"And keep a look-out in case you're spotted," said Surinder.

I nodded.

Sara and Surinder looked at each other. "Perhaps it's the only way to get him to stop talking about this imaginary pirate," said Sara.

"And get his mind back on football," added Surinder.

"We'll do it on Saturday morning at the end of my round," I grinned, and hurried away to football practice before they could change their minds.

Chapter Six

When Saturday arrived, I sneaked two pairs of Mum's bright-yellow rubber gloves from the cupboard under the sink, and stuffed them into my jacket pocket. Then I pedalled off to do my round.

Sara and Surinder were waiting for me at number 13 when I finally got there.

"This *is* a weird street," whispered Sara. "Some of the houses are very odd-looking."

"You should see some of the *people* who live in them," I said.

"Never mind that," hissed Surinder. "What do you want us to do?"

"You can help me search the bin while Sara keeps a look-out," I said, handing him a pair of rubber gloves.

"I hope no one sees me wearing these," he complained.

Sara stood under the chestnut tree while I put the paper under the stone by the front door, then Surinder and I tiptoed round to the back. The wheelie bin was in its usual place. Under the unblinking eye of the garden gnome, we crept towards it.

But we weren't the only ones there.

"Look, our first clue," I whispered excitedly, pointing to a long line of insects that were making their way up the path. "Weevils!"

"They're ants, you idiot," hissed Surinder.

I shrugged, opened the lid of the bin, and poked about among the pongy orange peel and eggshells. "There's just a load of rubbish in here," I said.

"What did you expect? A couple of wooden legs and a pirate flag?"

I ignored him as we rummaged through cat-food tins and bird-seed packets.

"There are no rum bottles, just a load of empty fish-finger boxes. What kind of a pirate eats fish fingers?"

"This kind," said a low, menacing voice.
Surinder and I both screamed.

A huge pirate loomed above us. He wore stripy black-and-white trousers tucked into high, black boots, a black jacket criss-crossed with silver chains, and a three-cornered hat. A thick, black beard covered his chin, and a vivid red scar was slashed across his cheek.

"Now what would you landlubbers be doin' here?" he snarled, putting his hands on his hips. "Are ye lookin' to steal Captain Cross-eyed's treasure? For if ye are I shall make ye walk the plank till ye fall SPLASH into a sea of hungry sharks. Oo-aarr!"

"N-n-n-no," I said. "We just…"

Then the pirate took off his beard and gave a hearty laugh. "Hello, Jonny Smith," he said. "Would you like to introduce me to your friend? *Friends*," he corrected, as Sara came running round the corner. "And then you can tell me why you are so interested in the contents of my bin."

I breathed a sigh of relief. So did Surinder.

"This is Sara and Surinder, and…" I paused.

"And?"

"And they didn't believe I had seen a pirate. Neither did my teacher, nor my dad, who said you gave him boxes of sausages for the children's summer barbeque. I was looking for clues in your bin to convince them."

"Aarr." Captain Cross-eyed put on his pirate's voice again. "Clues. Like ground-up bones and dead-men's chests, ye mean."

I gulped. I hadn't thought of that.

Captain Cross-eyed laughed. "I met your dad, Jonny, when he came to the factory to collect the sausages. He's a sensible man who will only believe the evidence of his own eyes. Why don't the three of you bring him here for a pirate tea, tomorrow at four o'clock."

Sara, Surinder and I looked at each other. A pirate tea? Wow!

"OK," we agreed.

Then we closed the lid of the bin, said goodbye to Captain Cross-eyed, and cycled back to my house.

Chapter Seven

Dad agreed to come to the pirate tea. He wanted to find out more about Captain Cross-eyed, too.

"There's just one small problem," said Mum, when she came home and heard about our invitation. "I need to go and visit Gran again, so you'll have to take Ellie with you."

"She'll eat all the pirate biscuits," I protested. "We'll be left with the weevils." But it was no use. Ellie still had to come.

❧

Sara and Surinder were leaning on their bikes by the big chestnut tree at number 13 when Mum dropped us off the next day.

"I'll pick you up on my way back from Gran's," she said. "Have fun!"

Dad hobbled behind us as we walked down the path. When we neared the front door, it slowly creaked open. A large pirate stood there. Out of one black sleeve gleamed a shiny metal hook. He held it up in greeting.

"I be Captain Cross-eyed," he boomed. "Welcome aboard. Oo-aarr."

"Er… Hi," we all said. Apart from Ellie. She pointed up at him. "Pi," she said.

We laughed and went inside.

"Wow!" I breathed, when we entered the sitting room. It didn't look like the one we have at home. It was like walking into a *real* pirate ship!

Captain Cross-eyed grinned as we gazed around, our mouths open.

Two of the walls were covered in rigging, which I just itched to climb. A fantastic bookcase made out of driftwood filled another wall, while curtains made from shells and seaweed hung at the window. There were even tables and chairs made out of old barrels.

"Look," Surinder nudged me. "That table's got GUNPOWDER stencilled on the side."

On the window ledge a one-eared cat snoozed, totally ignoring the parrot that danced about from foot to foot cackling, "Walk the plank, matey. Walk the plank."

Captain Cross-eyed held up his hook and the parrot flew onto it. "This is Olly," he smiled. "He's a terrible thief. Watch your pockets or he'll pinch your money."

"Pieces of eight. Pieces of eight," cackled Olly.

But it was the fourth wall that really interested me. It was covered with portraits of fierce-looking pirates. They didn't look a bit like our family, though Gran can be a bit grumpy sometimes.

Captain Cross-eyed followed my gaze. "Some of my ancestors were pirates," he explained. "Let's have tea and I'll tell you all about them."

I couldn't wait.

We sat around the big gunpowder table.

Olly hopped on to my shoulder. I could feel his sharp claws through my sweater and, when he moved, his soft feathers tickled my cheek.

The cat, who was called Scarface Jack, turned out to be a real softie, and let Ellie stroke his head. I just hoped she wouldn't nibble his one remaining ear.

"Have a dead-men's-eyes biscuit, Jonny," smiled Captain Cross-eyed, holding out a large scallop-shell plate.

I took one and had a nibble. Then I took a bigger bite. Dead-men's-eyes biscuits tasted like chocolate-chip cookies to me.

After that, we had black-spot cakes. They had a chocolate button on the top, and were just like my mum's fairy cakes. Then, according to Captain Cross-eyed, we washed it all down with the blood of an ancient mariner. Funny how their blood tasted the same as Coke.

When we were full, Captain Cross-eyed sat back and started to tell us all about the portraits. "That's Captain Cross-fingers," he said, pointing to a black-bearded pirate. "He was a great storyteller and could weave fantastic tales. But he also told enormous porkies, which got him into lots of trouble."

"Like some of your excuses for being late, Jonny," grinned Surinder.

"Shush," I nudged him, in case Dad heard.

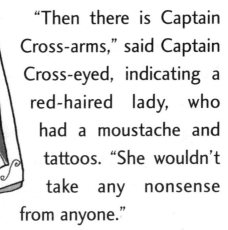

"Then there is Captain Cross-arms," said Captain Cross-eyed, indicating a red-haired lady, who had a moustache and tattoos. "She wouldn't take any nonsense from anyone."

"Sounds a bit like Miss Dodds," said Sara.

"Looks a bit like Miss Dodds, too," I grinned.

"Who's the chap with the treasure map?" asked Dad.

"Ah," said Captain Cross-eyed. "That's Captain Cross. He was a grumpy old man, but brilliant at reading maps. He found lots of treasure, usually other people's, which he pinched."

"I've met loads of people like that in my job," said Dad. "I broke my leg chasing a bunch of thieves."

"But at least that's exciting," said Captain Cross-eyed. "The chasing bit, I mean, not the broken leg. My job's not exciting at all. Nothing much ever happens in the sausage factory. I'd love to be a pirate like my ancestors, but there's not much call for them these days." He looked so sad that Ellie, who had been climbing on and off the little barrel tables with Scarface Jack, came over and offered him her pink rabbit.

That made Captain Cross-eyed smile. Then he got out his tin whistle and played some pirate tunes for Olly to dance to.

All too soon, Mum arrived to take us home. We said goodbye to Captain Cross-eyed, waved Sara and Surinder off on their bikes, and got into the car.

My mind was in a whirl with everything I'd seen.

"You're very quiet, Jonny," said Mum. "Didn't you enjoy the pirate tea?"

"Tea," said Ellie, before I could reply. "Tea."

"You've just had tea, Ellie," said Mum. "You can't be hungry."

"Actually, she didn't eat anything at all," said Dad. "She was too busy playing."

I'd noticed that, too. Which was why I was being so quiet. My brain was working overtime. Ellie had enjoyed playing in the pirate house, and Captain Cross-eyed really wanted to be more like his pirate ancestors. I smiled. I thought I might just know a way to help them both...

Chapter Eight

On Sunday night, when I was supposed to be doing my homework, I drew a picture of all the things that were buzzing through my head. I put the picture into my rucksack and showed it to Sara and Surinder the next day.

"A big pirate ship in the park!" they exclaimed. "That would be great."

"I'm sure Captain Cross-eyed could set it up," I said. "And look, we could have all sorts of activities, like rope climbing and…"

"Walking the plank," said Surinder.

"Fighting off enemy ships," said Sara.

"Hammock swinging," said Surinder.

"Treasure hunting," said Sara.

I grinned. They were getting the idea.

Later, Dad got the idea, too. "A pirate ship with pirate activities?" he said thoughtfully. "That would certainly be fun for the children round here. It would keep them fit, too."

"It would let Captain Cross-eyed be a real pirate, like his ancestors."

Dad smiled. "And give me something to organise while I'm off work with this broken leg. Good thinking, son." Then he hobbled off, whistling, to make a few phone calls.

"Well done," whispered Mum. "I haven't seen your dad so cheerful in ages."

A few days went by and Dad was so busy we hardly saw him. Then he announced that he and I were going back to visit Captain Cross-eyed. "We have some pirate matters to discuss," he grinned.

The captain was just polishing off his tea of fish fingers when we arrived.

"I hate sausages," he grinned. "What can I do for you?"

"Tell him, Jonny," said Dad.

I explained my idea about the pirate ship in the park.

Captain Cross-eyed looked doubtful. "It sounds wonderful, but…"

"Dad thinks it can be done," I said.

"Over the last week I've spoken to a lot of people who are willing to help," nodded Dad. "The council, local businesses, parents… They all think it's a fantastic idea."

"I would love to do it," said Captain Cross-eyed. "The children could take part in all kinds of activities, even sword fights. We'd use wooden swords, of course. And we could have barrels to crawl through and climb over and…"

Captain Cross-eyed had got the idea, too. Then he and Dad sat down and made lists of all the things they would need to set it up while I played with Olly and Scarface Jack.

"How did Scarface Jack lose his ear?"
I asked. "I bet it was in a fight with another
pirate cat. I bet the other cat slunk away
when he realised that Scarface Jack would
fight to the death, even if he only had one
ear, or one eye, or one paw left."

"It might have been like that," grinned
Captain Cross-eyed. "Or he might have
been born with only one ear, and I might
have got him from the cat rescue centre
because no one else wanted him. But that
could be our secret. I like your story better."

I liked Captain Cross-eyed.

I also liked the speed at which my dad got things done. Before long, there was a lot of hammering and banging going on in the park. A big, wooden pirate ship took shape, with rope ladders snaking down its sides and a Jolly Roger flag fluttering at its mast. The name *Silver Arrow* was painted on its prow, and a large plank fixed near the stern.

"We're going to put a big paddling pool filled with plastic balls and sharks underneath," grinned Captain Cross-eyed.

෴

Mr McGregor, our football coach, was the first to notice what was going on. "I saw your dad yesterday when I was out on my run," he said to me at football practice. "He says there's a pirate activity centre being set up. Said it was your idea. Is that right?"

I nodded.

"Well done, laddie. Soon as it's ready, I'll be along there with the football team. Make a change from the usual training."

Then Mr Maini mentioned it to me. "I'm putting up a notice in my shop window about the big pirate ship in the park. It seems a Captain Cross-eyed, whom I know as Mr Cross, is to be in charge of it. Seems you weren't telling silly stories after all. I owe you an apology."

"That's O.K., Mr Maini," I grinned. "It *was* all rather strange."

Only Miss Dodds didn't mention it. Not even when the big pirate ship opened and news of it was in the local paper.

Everyone from miles around went to the opening dressed as a pirate, though Dad wasn't too pleased when I called him Peg Leg.

Captain Cross-eyed looked fantastic. He stood at the ship's wheel in his full pirate outfit. "Welcome aboard!" he cried. "Everyone must have fun or my name's not Captain Cross-eyed." Then he crossed his eyes and made people laugh.

Not to be outdone, Olly hopped about cackling. "Where's the treasure? Where's the treasure?" And tried to poke his beak into people's pockets.

Everyone had a wonderful time, especially Captain Cross-eyed. "I'm a real pirate at last," he grinned. "And it's all thanks to you, Jonny." Then he put his hand into his pocket and handed me a large coin. "It's a gold doubloon. Your dad was telling me you're saving up to buy a new bike." And before I could thank him, he strode off to show two girls how to have a proper sword fight.

Dad was really pleased at how well everything had gone, too. "I'm sorry I thought the idea of a pirate in Weir Street was nonsense," he said.

"That's all right," I grinned, "because I've got something else tell you. Captain Cross-eyed's not the only strange person to live in Weird Street. Guess who lives at number 34 and a half..."

WeirDStreet

Just how weird can the people in Weir Street be?
Join Jonny on *all* his adventures…

WeirDStreet

The Curse of
Captain Cross-eyed
Margaret Ryan

WeirDStreet

The Treasure of Mr Tipp
Margaret Ryan

WeirDStreet

The Riddle of Dr Sphinx
Margaret Ryan

WeirDStreet

The Mystery of Miss King
Margaret Ryan